Between the Lines

Between the Lines

Pam Line

Chapeltown Books

British Library Cataloguing in Publication Data

A Record of this Publication is available from the British Library

ISBN 978-1-910542-68-2

This edition published 2021 by Chapeltown Books
Manchester, England

Contents

Introduction

Life is full of interesting and wonderful stories. Every day a page turns to reveal nature in its quirkiest forms. Chance encounters, happy events and tragedy mix into a melange of experiences. This anthology is an attempt to capture truth, possibly somewhat exaggerated, and shows our daily lives in a pared-down fashion, in snippets that appear important with a sheen of incredulity. Most of these tales are true, some even verbatim. I hope that you enjoy reading them.

Pam Line

Lucia

On arrival in Rome the train edged along the platform. A man took his crutches and helped him down the steps. The Italians were deferential to American uniforms.

Christ, he needed a drink before he met Lucia. She had become a burden. After the blood of battle he needed to breathe; she wouldn't allow that. Lucia smothered him. The two months he had known her were turning into a life sentence. His head buzzed after their argument, which had turned into a noisy scene of flashing teeth and talons.

He found himself outside a bar. The windows ran with condensation, and the ragtime was loud. He could see a sailor. The girl on his lap wore his hat.

He pushed towards the bar and ordered. The glass slid along the bar, spilling some of the Bourbon. The drops sparkled on the zinc counter.

A brunette sashayed by. He caught her arm and she smiled.

Ciao, Bella… Addio, Lucia.

Tottenham Boy

I was born on 1st January 1998 in the nick. My mother had been banged up for killing my father. If he was my father, that is, I'd so many 'uncles' I bet she wasn't sure either.

She was up the duff with me in them days, and they say my father was a right bastard. On the social he was, and the booze, and a kiddie fiddler to boot, so they say. He'd landed back at the gaff, well oiled, and she started shouting. 'Get away from me, you filthy pig.' Yer know, stuff like she always shouted when he came back slaughtered. My nan told me my mother was standing with her back to the sink, the mucky pots piled high. She were a slut and still is. He went for her, clocked her one in the mouth, she reached behind, grabbed a knife, and sank it deep in his belly. 'Yer bloody whore,' he gasped as he keeled over, and that was the end of him. Even the cat smiled.

The Beak must have been sorry for her, with broken teeth, a black eye, and about to drop, 'cause he said, 'In the circumstances, with due provocation, I sentence you to three years in prison.' Well, the old bag, my mother, fainted. The screws had to carry her down to the meat wagon with her screaming, 'It's coming, open the door, you bloody narks, the pain, the pain, I demand my rights, get me a doctor.' That was all cobblers, as she had kids like shelling peas. She thought I was the eighth, but wasn't that sure.

They took me to live with my nan. Grandad had legged it with a trollop years before. Nan lived by reading fortunes with tea leaves, she was good at making up what her customers wanted to hear.

When my mother came out of the nick, she came to live with us in Ferry Lane. She was having bong sessions with her mates nearly every day, so she didn't know where she was half the time. She never said my name unless it was, 'Come here, Tommy, yer little bastard, else I'll hit yer.' I wished they'd kept her in the nick, it would have been safer for everybody.

Next door was a nest of gangsters. Me and their youngest lad, Billy, were best mates. We was meant to go to school when we was five but we didn't see why we had to learn stupid things like reading and sums. The Filth came round sometimes and made us go. We wouldn't speak to the teachers, so they left us alone. Right lot of turnips they were. Told us we didn't have a chance unless we knuckled down to some work.

Billy and me did all sorts of things, like going to the park and catapulting birds. Once we caught a duck and Billy hit it with a brick. My nan said that next time we should wring its neck 'cause we made a mess of it, and it were tough.

Billy's Uncle Jim sold drugs and stolen stuff. We did deliveries for him and picked things up, earning money for cider and fags. Camden market was a good place for nicking handbags, but by that time we were sixteen and we had to be careful not to get nicked ourselves.

That summer, Billy's uncle got killed by The Scum. They said he had a gun, but he hadn't. Billy and me watched it on the telly. At first, the police were trying to hold back the crowds. Then people broke through and started running and shouting. It was exciting. There was knock on the door, I took off the chain, and someone screamed, 'Come on, Currys' front has been smashed in. We've got some trolleys from Waitrose, move yer arses.'

It was a hot night. We ran towards the crowds, grabbed a trolley and piled it with gear. I thought if I gave my mother the microwave she might leave me alone.

The next night was the same. We'd just got up the Tottenham Court Road when a carpet shop went up in flames. It were amazing watching it burn. The computer shop caught fire too. Billy shouted, 'I'm going in for an iPad.' Before I could stop him, he'd disappeared into the smoke.

He was the only person I'd ever loved, or who had loved me. I couldn't let him burn.

Day Trip

Esther and Marie, from Liversedge, on a day out to Morecambe, on the beach, breeze blowing, seagulls screeching. Transistor radio playing Here Comes Summer. Sea slapping on the sand, children shouting and laughing.

MARIE: I thought that bus were never going to get here. [*Sound of bags being put down, being unzipped, rustling of paper*] It must have stopped fifty times between Bradford and Morecambe, and why the driver had to have a half hour in Preston is beyond me. I don't like lingering in Lancashire.

ESTHER: Ee, you and the War of the Roses! A good job we won, that's all I can say.

MARIE: A good job the weather's alright or else it wouldn't have been worth setting off. [Shouting to the children] Dorcas, don't go too far out in the sea, the water's too cold for me to do a rescue job. [Pause] Esther, stop looking at that lifeguard and give us an 'and with this rug.

[*Sounds of a child running, ice cream van chimes*]

1st CHILD: Mum, Mum, can we have an ice cream? Please, please, you said we could.

MARIE: Flipping heck, we've only just landed. I haven't got my breath back, go away, shoo.

1st CHILD: Aw, meanie.

MARIE: Just go away, else you'll get nowt.

1st CHILD: [*Running away shouting*] You're horrible, I never get anything.'

MARIE: Little darlings. Right, lass, with a bit of luck we should get some peace and quiet for at least five minutes. What are you reading?

ESTHER: Robyn Carr.

MARIE: You were reading that last time we were here.

ESTHER: No, it was a different one of hers. I love a love story, like you and Frank. Go on, tell me again, tell me about when you first met Frank.

MARIE: You're as bad as the kids, want, want, can I, can I. Do you want some coffee?

ESTHER: Mmm, yes please.

[*Sound of thermos being unscrewed, pouring of coffee*]

ESTHER: Go on then.

MARIE: What?

ESTHER: Tell me about you and Frank

MARIE: I've told you before.

ESTHER: I know, but I never get tired of hearing it.

MARIE: Well, I don't really like talking about it, although these days my past doesn't matter, Frank says.

ESTHER: He's such a lovely man, I wish I'd met him first. Go on, tell me again.

MARIE: Well I were up Manningham Lane, working like—

ESTHER: [*Cutting in*] I remember that bit.

MARIE: A girl's got to make a living, and suddenly there he was, and he said, 'It's a cold night, could I buy you a coffee?' I was gobsmacked. He didn't want aught else. [*Dreamily*] We just sat and talked in the Alassio coffee bar. Do you remember it? It was down t'steps near the Alhambra. Talked for hours about Bradford, how it was changing, what it was like when we were growing up. Do you know, all the time, he lived only two streets away, in Little Germany. Of course, we weren't allowed to mix with them in those days.

ESTHER: You haven't told me that before. What do you mean, not allowed to mix?

MARIE: Hang on a minute. [*Shouts*] Hey, our Rachel, come back here, what are you doing with that bucket?

[*Pause, a child's voice shouts*]

13

CHILD: She took my crab.

MARIE: What?

CHILD: She took my crab.

MARIE: Stop it. You can't do that just because she stole yer crab.

CHILD: It were a big 'un.

MARIE: It doesn't matter if it was a big 'un, stop clattering her with your bucket. You're eight, and she's only three. [*Raising her voice*] If you don't stop now we're off back to the bus station and, when we get back, I'll tell your dad. [*Aside to Esther, dreamily*] He'll just stroke her hair and tell her a story about sharing and caring. I says to him, she's bonny but a bit of a handful. He says she's an angel. Why am I saying this? Where were we? Oh yes, we weren't allowed to mix. You see Frank's Jewish. For my dad it was worse than being a Catholic. My dad said you should never mix outside your own sort. He died before I met Frank. He wouldn't have liked him. Too good to be real, he'd have said. Mother thinks he's God's own gift. So do I.

ESTHER: [*Shouting*] Hey, our Liz, don't go in too deep, I'm not taking my clothes off to fetch you. [*Aside to Marie*] Since the operation, it looks like I've got a bum at the front. [*Shouting again*] And keep your eye on Dorcas. [*To Marie*] Those surgeons are nearly all men. I've told you what he said before he chopped my bits off?

14

MARIE: Yes, but go on. You could have missed a bit last time you told me.

[*Shuffling on the sand, making herself more comfortable*]

ESTHER: He said, 'Mrs Everard, you have a polyp in your right breast and I am going to cut away a slice so the cancer doesn't spread.' I just burst into tears, after all I was only twenty six, it was like having my feminininity – is that right? – violated. Then he said, 'If this had happened ten years ago, I would have taken the lot off.' But I must say, after speaking to your Frank, a weight lifted off my shoulders. He said that it's me that matters, and that if having t'operation put blokes off, they weren't worth it anyway.

MARIE: [*Shouting*] Jordan, bring the baby back, he needs more sun oil. Hey, just look at that, Esther, just see how she sweeps him up in her arms and cradles him, his tiny hand resting on her shoulder like a starfish. She looks like a painting that Frank showed me at the cathedral in Durham. It were called Madonna and Child.

ESTHER: What, her with that black baby, the one she adopted from Africa?

MARIE: No, you dozy mare, Mary Madonna, mother of Jesus.

ESTHER: Sorry, it's just that these days, what with The Sun and Hello magazine, she seems more important than Mary, and she did sing that song called Like a Virgin. The other one, I remember her from confirmation lessons, she were a good woman.

15

MARIE: Frank says that no one can be sure she wasn't a fallen woman. Jesus's mother that is. After all, Joseph didn't seem to know about her being in the family way. Later in life Jesus met a woman called Mary Magdalene. She was definitely fallen and he forgave her. I've thought about it a lot. [*Shouting*] Our Jordan, come here, our Christopher is going to burn without more cream.

[*Childish squeak in the background*]

CHILD: Aw, Mum.

MARIE: Never mind *aw Mum*. Forget the sandcastle, it'll keep, the tide's going out.

ESTHER: If you talk with the young girls that have been married a year or two, they're having trouble keeping their men at home. There's temptation everywhere. The web, it's a perverts' paradise. [*Pause*] Did I tell you the other day I decided to get another cat and typed in 'Persian kittens', and what do you think it came up with? A site that encouraged me to join by showing women in very strange positions. Thank the Lord my John hasn't seen it, or else he'd have me swinging from the top of the wardrobe. [*Shouting*] Elizabeth, do not stick your tongue out just because someone wants to borrow your spade for a moment, and look after Dorcas, she's eating sand.

MARIE: Come here, you two and give me a hug. Come on Dorcas, Lizzie, let's have a big love. Then you kids can bury Esther and me up to our necks.

SMALL CHILD: Yippee. If we dig deep enough, we'll get to Austria.

ANOTHER SMALL VOICE: Durrbrain, Australia.

MARIE: I wonder how the lads are getting on with the wedding at Carnforth?

ESTHER: I'm sure things will be OK with Frank in charge, although John was worried that there might not be enough wine. You know they're Romanians? John called to see them yesterday to check on the time and place. They've been here only a couple of months, and the house they're living in is awful. They're paying through the nose for a hovel.

MARIE: Don't worry Esther, Frank will have sorted the wine out. They should be finished by now, so they'll be here soon.

ESTHER: Yes, he's wonderful. He always thinks about other people before himself. [*Shouting*] Dorcas, you'll be poorly if you drink seawater and, no, the hole isn't deep enough for Marie and me to get buried. Keep on digging.

MARIE: Yes, he's wonderful but I wish he wouldn't show off.

ESTHER: He's not like that, he's just lovely.

MARIE: OK, who's that walking towards us on the water?

The Banks

The cirrus clouds were motionless, the sun and sky scorching, everyone de-coated after a grey unremitting winter. It was March 25th, and that night the clocks would spring forwards towards the optimistic heat of a long summer. Such are the expectations of Northerners. It was probably a blip, but the world and his wife were out making the most of it. Sandra and I joined them.

The dogs ran and rollicked, barking at the horses in the field and anything else that looked like fun. The newly installed half-tree, hooligan-proof bench beckoned. Ilkley Moor and distant Haworth were already coming into view – as was Deirdre.

Deirdre, chairperson of the committee, was the self-appointed warden who made sure that people behaved themselves on The Banks. The land had secured village green status and Deirdre rigidly stuck to the rules and regulations. She was heading in our direction.

'I've just found someone reading a mucky magazine.' she spluttered. 'I told him what I thought and he actually told me to bugger off! How rude.'

Deirdre turned on her heel, and walked off without waiting for a response.

'Oh bother,' wailed Sandra.

'What's up, lass?' I asked, in my best Yorkshire.

'Some blokes are sat on our bench.'

That's alright. I'll ask them to move up.'

There were two lads, fortyish.

'Go on, shove up then.'

'Suit yourselves. we're having a drink.' They shuffled up the bench.

The one at the far end pushed a litre bottle of sherry under his armpit, with the neck stuck out. The second one had a different poison, a litre bottle of Cinzano in a bag. They were both three sheets to the wind. The first one had the most amazing electric blue eyes rimmed with black eyelashes. The second one was pale, fair-haired, and kindly looking.

'Don't mind what you do, as long as you don't frighten the horses.'

Blue Eyes stopped mid-slurp, looking around frantically. 'What 'orses?'

'Dozy bugger,' murmured his mate.

Sandra and I exchanged glances, trying not to laugh.

'Lovely day, do you live round here?'

'Yep, just down there,' replied the Fair One. He pointed down to Queensway, the road that runs through a huge council estate towards Guiseley.

'I'm from Pudsey.' said Blue Eyes.

'Ah, where the crows fly backwards over the treacle mines.'

'Yer what?'

'Fancy not knowing your own history.'

I couldn't look at Sandra, I knew that she would be trying desperately not to guffaw, the same as me.

The four of us sat in silence for a moment, two of us taking in the view, the other two swigging more hooch.

A lady walked past with two large, white, shaggy dogs.

'What sort are they?' asked Blue Eyes. A haze of Cinzano wafted over from him and he gave a spectacular burp. 'Oops, sorry.'

'Salukis,' said Sandra.

Blue Eyes stood unsteadily and clicked his heels together.

'What are yer doing?' said Cinzano.

'Someone said salute.'

'Sit down, you clart arse.'

Blue Eyes slumped back down onto the bench. In the same movement he managed to unscrew the bottle for another gulp to steady his nerves.

'The Germans landed in Pudsey during t'war,' mused Blue Eyes.

'Don't be so daft. The only Germans that landed in England were shot down.'

'Hey you, yes you, the blonde one, if they didn't land in Pudsey, how come I found a German helmet and a boot when I was a kid?'

'They must have dropped out of a plane when they came over to bomb the airport and hit Bradford instead.'

'Oh yes, flying upside down were they? Just look it up on your phone. I'm right, my Mam told me. I'm right. You're not that smart. Heh, do you want a rollie?'

'Yes please.'

Blue Eyes passed over the pouch of tobacco and the papers, winked at Cinzano and whispered, 'Bet she can't roll one.' He took another swig of his sherry.

I rolled the fag and he passed over the lighter.

'Bloody 'ell… not just a pretty face are yer?'

'Actually, I am trying to give them up.'

'Oh God, are you going to blame me?'

For one awful moment I thought he was going to stand up and put his arms around me, but his legs weren't up to the task.

'What's your dog?' he asked.

'A Bichon Frise.'

'Is it a rescue dog?'

'Yes, someone had to have it.'

'What's its name?

'Blossom.'

'It looks like that dog in Silence of the Lambs. That was called Blossom. Do you remember? They put it in a bowl to skin it.'

'No, I didn't see the film. I'm not keen on Anthony Hopkins.'

'Who's he? Did they skin it? I can't remember. Fancy you calling it Blossom.'

A Jet 2 plane roared into view, cutting the azure sky with a hazy vapour trail.

'That's the 4.15 to Gdansk.'

'Where the fuck's Gdansk?'

'Have another drink, numptie.'

'I'd a dog once, when I was a kid. It were called Rover but the feasties took it. Bet you don't know what a feastie is?'

'Could be a gypsy?'

'Well sort of… it's the gypsies what come with fairs. Them what bring roundabouts and stalls where you can net a goldfish that allus dies the next day. It's them what took Rover, my Mam said so.'

I was hoping against hope that Deirdre wouldn't come back this way.

My musing was broken by Blue Eyes. 'I had a dog called Daisy too.'

'What breed was it?'

'I don't know, but it looked like Lassie.'

'A Collie?'

'I've never heard of that, but that's what it looked like. It were seventeen when it were killed.'

'So sorry. What happened to it?'

'It were run over by a Robin Reliant.'

Sandra and I had done well to bottle the mirth up for so long, but this was too much. We burst into peals of hysterical giggles. Blue Eyes was cross.

'It's a good job I've got over it or you would have been sorry, laughing like that. She was a bonny dog.'

'Did it have three tyre marks over it? Was it Del Boy what dunnit?'

At this, Blue Eyes cackled.

'Aye, it did.' He smiled, raised the bottle to his lips and drank deeply.

It was time to go before Deirdre caught us fraternising with a couple of alcoholics.

The Mistake

Bloody NHS, got me in a real twist. Why did they say 'yes'? I'm sixty-six years old and in a right mess. I hope he reads this. That surgeon, he wants prosecuting. Problem was that I couldn't get it up, yer know, todger. T'wife wasn't interested any road, but it bothered me.

I went to the doctor. Nice man, he's Chinese, speaks decent English in a 'velly well' kind of way.

He said, 'Well, Mr Hardcastle, have you tried Viagra?'

And I said to him, 'I've tried everything. Viagra, porn, and amyl nitrate from the sex shop, although that made me dizzy. I even tried a massage parlour, but t'lass could do nowt.

'Mr Hardcastle,' he said. 'With penile dysfunction we can fit you with a pump, but there is no guarantee.'

'I'll try owt.' I said.

So, they did. And it was alright for a while. Then I got to thinking that women have a better time than me, and that I was in the wrong body. So, back I went to Doctor Wang.

He said, 'This is somewhat out of my remit. I will make an appointment for you to speak to a psychologist.'

So, I did. The psychologist said, 'Have you thought about the effect on your family and friends?'

And I said, 'Yes, long and hard, and they all agree with me.'

So, they did it. Now I've got tits, the whole business. But it hasn't made me happy. People laugh at my big hands and deep voice. They are treating me for depression, but they can't turn me back to what I was – a silly old codger.

The Palace Hotel

On the beach I watch the warning beacon at the end of the headland. It reminds me of the war, searchlight fingers feeling the sky for German planes. What I am doing feels like war too, the need for subterfuge and cunning.

A hoary haar sweeps in from the North Sea, flicking sand in my face. As I attempt to light a cigarette with a Zippo lighter, memories of the person who gave it to me cloud my mind.

The tide is on the ebb. The sea throws white horses at the moss-encrusted groynes, whispers, and shushes back to her deep corner, an analogy for what I feel like at home – washed up, deeply unhappy and unwanted.

I take a walk along the beach, heading towards The Esplanade. My footsteps fill with water as they trail behind me in the newly scoured sand. The sun dips below the horizon, and street lights thicken the darkness out towards Belgium. Maybe that is where I will go. Get away from the constant sadness that takes my head to dark places, the taunts of, 'You'll never leave me, you know which side your bread is buttered.' He'll believe it tomorrow when he realises I've cleared out his bank account.

I lift my bag from the boot of the car and walk towards the welcoming arms of the Palace Hotel. Above it, the castle is an eerie skeleton in the gloom.

The Palace is still grand, although somewhat faded these days. I visited as a child with my Edwardian parents. Back then, conversation at dinner revolved around the war.

In '39 the doors were opened by a flunky dressed as a character from The Mikado, with lots of gold braid and tassels. With a reverential bow, he waved guests regally towards the reception desk. Today the hotel still has grand pretensions, rather like a dowager duchess fallen on hard times. The doors slide open mechanically, the staircase sweeps upwards with a gleaming banister, the carpet is somewhat shabby. Rather than a Palm Court Trio regaling clients with Glenn Miller's Moonlight Serenade, anodyne piped music wraps itself around the marble columns. Crystal chandeliers spill facets of light, twinkling promises of the evening to come.

I check into the hotel using our joint credit card.

The receptionist points to the lift rather than taking me to it. My instructions regarding the time of dinner and breakfast, and when I am expected to vacate the room, are delivered in a bored tone that implies he is between jobs as a mogul of industry, not a desk clerk.

Sifting through my wardrobe at home, I had settled on the Yves Saint Laurent 'le smoking' suit, with black, patent leather boots. When I look in the mirror, my hair is a trifle too long, curling over the collar of my jacket. I shoot my cuffs and I'm ready to meet the hordes determined on a good time.

I sit in the Fun Bar, waiting for the barman to serve me a Black Russian cocktail.

Couples are milling about, meeting friends, laughing. Maybe one day I'll meet somebody, and be happy again, but it will take time to get over Gregory's infidelity.

Over the hubbub an announcement comes via the tinny tannoy.

'Dinner will be served in ten minutes. The seating plan is in the foyer. Only three hours to go before Big Ben strikes us into the New Year. Are we going to enjoy ourselves?'

Cheers ring out from the dinner-suited men and their partners in strapless frilly frocks, as they move towards the foyer.

I have been placed with someone named Alice, at a corner table for two, well away from the sprung dance floor.

'Hello Alice, what brings you here?'

'It's a welcome change from living with Mother. I'm recently divorced and I can't find a good apartment. *C'est la vie*, as they say in France. Something will turn up.'

'I'm separated from my husband, divorce to follow.'

Waiters ply between the tables delivering bottles of Dom Perignon. I order a bottle and when it arrives I pour a glass for Alice.

We clink glasses.

'What happened with your marriage, if you don't mind me asking?'

'He left me for the postman,' Alice said. 'Makes a change from a younger woman.'

'It would seem that we have something in common. Mine opted for his personal trainer.'

Alice giggles, I see her perfect teeth, her tongue teasing, although I'm sure that she is unaware of the effect she is having. Or is she?

The glitter ball spins, making the dancers jerky like an old black and white movie.

'Alice, would you like a cigarette?'

She shakes her head. Blonde curls touch her bare shoulders.

I put a black Sobranie into my cigarette holder, light it with the Zippo and have another glass of champagne.

Couples dance to Tragedy by the Bee Gees, some hopping from one foot to the other, others getting down to The Twist.

'Alice, before the Black Forest cherry gateau arrives, would you care to dance?'

On the dance floor I take Alice in my arms. The crowd opens like the Red Sea. Do we look a strange couple? I don't care.

We dance all night, cutting a dash on the floor. After a second bottle of Dom Perignon I feel like John Travolta twirling Olivia Newton John in Saturday Night Fever.

Alice is beautiful.

It is five minutes to midnight. People are gathering round the edges of the ballroom, ready to sing Auld Lang Syne.

'Alice, would you like to go to Belgium?'

'When?'

'Tomorrow.'

'The day after would be better.'

I cock a mental snook at Gregory. Being with Alice is going to be much more fun than being Mrs Gregory Huntington Smythe.

Cruising with Pam, My Lovely Daughter

It's lovely this cruising lark, but I'll be glad of a rest.

When Harry was alive, I thought it was an easy way of holidaying, but not these days. You get saluted on board, and escorted to your cabin by a lovely looking boy from Malaysia or somewhere else exotic. He empties your suitcase, hangs things up, and makes sure there is plenty of soap and toilet rolls, that sort of thing, all for a tip. In the old days, the stewards used to bring cups of tea whenever you wanted, but now it's a kettle and those fiddly milk pots that I can't open. Every night when you get back from the show, he's twisted towels into extraordinary shapes, gorillas, swans, elephants, you name it, just to amuse and keep up your spirits. However, they don't lay out your nightie any longer or put a rose on your pillow.

Though he did something the other day which I wasn't too happy about. I'd left my undies on the bed, meaning to rinse them through later, and when I got back to the cabin he'd washed them and hung them up to dry. Well, I mean, would you like someone interfering with your privates? In the old days, they would never have dreamt of touching them. Harry would have been upset.

I grumbled about it to Pam. Pam is my daughter, who's accompanying me under sufferance. She'd rather be doing something 'educashunnal', something that stretches the mind a bit further than what time the sun rises over the yardarm for the first drink of the day.

'Pam,' I said, 'I think that was beyond the call of duty.'

'What's that?' she said.

'Washing out my smalls.'

Well you should have seen her face. It was that uppitty look, the one she reserves for anyone she thinks is pointless.

'Goodness, mother', she said. 'Not those horrible hospital knickers. Not only does he deserve a tip, but a medal too!'

She doesn't seem to realise that, at my age, comfort is of supreme importance. How she wears those bits of string and lace, I have no idea. It's a good job we're not all alike.

So, there is nothing to do, only hop off and on, or in my case shuffle off and on, when we're in port. When the boat stops, everyone starts queuing to get off to go on trips. The ship is enough for me. It's nice when they've all gone. I can stretch out on the deck and enjoy a small sherry, like Harry and I used to do.

Harry loved cruising, he felt free on the open sea. He'd been in the tank regiment. After the war was over, he never went to the pictures unless he could get an aisle seat because he suffered from claustrophobia. Looking back, who could blame him? He had the Bosch in front, and probably behind as well, and he was stuck in the middle in a thing like a huge reinforced dustbin that either carried you across a minefield or it was goodnight Vienna.

I don't see any point going ashore, these places are all the same anyway. One year Pam and I went all the way up the Amazon to a place called Manaus and what did we find but a branch of C&A, long defunct in Leeds but still going strong in the Brazilian jungle. I ask you, what is the point? We could just as easily have gone to the shops in Leeds rather than go through all that discomfort, lots of flies and a nasty wet heat that made me break out in lumps.

Why is cruising not easy? I'll tell you. The ship is like a block of flats with seventeen decks. I still have no idea which is the front end. There's a shopping mall that is a small version of the White Rose Centre in Leeds, with gold lifts that shoot up and down in every corner. And the people! They're what I call 'bay window', all front and nothing behind. You can tell they're not used to the finer things in life, the way they flaunt their jewellery. I think most of it is bling, not like mine, a five-stone diamond eternity ring that Harry bought for me when we'd been married for a year.

Every night on the main deck they have a stall selling handbags, china ornaments, and things like that. The women, not ladies by any stretch of the imagination, wade in as though they are all prop forwards with the Bradford Bulls. It's a full scrummage to see who can buy the most tat. Goodness knows what their homes are like, probably identical homages to the Pound Shop.

This morning, after breakfast, my daughter adopted a loud voice. 'Connie.' she began. She calls me that when she's exasperated. 'I'm going behind the scenes at the AL HAM BRA.'

'What's that about your bra?'

She didn't reply. She speaks to me like that. I know I'm a bit deaf, but she talks as though I'm a bit daft as well.

31

'I'll collect you from the bridge club at 11 o'clock.' she said. 'Do you know how to get there?'

'Yes,' I lied. I wasn't going to tell her I hadn't got my bearings.

That's where I've been, on the bridge. I'm exhausted. After she left to go to the Alhambra, which I've since found out is the name of the theatre, I spied a nice looking young man wearing a peaked cap, with shiny shoes. I have always thought you can trust someone that polishes their shoes.

'Excuse me, but which way is it to the bridge?' I asked.

To which he replied, 'Sit down, Madam, I won't be a moment.' and took out his mobile phone. He chattered away for ages in some foreign language and I was getting a bit agitated. Anyway, he finished on the telephone and said that he would personally escort me to the bridge. We started walking up and down corridors. It was a bit like Bradford Infirmary.

He said, 'Have you been on the bridge before?' I told him I play twice a week. At that remark he seemed somewhat taken aback.

'Are you talking about boats?'

'No, cards.' said I, and we both laughed.

At that moment we both realised that we weren't on a short cut to the bridge club. We were on our way to The Bridge. Well, I thought, we're nearly there, so I might as well have a look round.

There was a lovely view from up there. It was like being in charge of the sea, the way the ship ploughed through the water. I met the captain, a nice enough chap. He was Danish, going to fat a bit like their bacon.

'Where's the wheel and the chair?' I asked.

'Madame, ships don't have a wheel any longer, and I don't have a parrot either.' We had a good laugh about that.

I like it when they call me Madame. It befits my status as an old and, I like to think, stately person. Of course, my daughter thinks I'm just doddery.

'Stride out,' she keeps saying. 'Stride out, Mother.'

I say to her, 'I'm frightened of falling over.'

Then she says, 'You're more likely to fall over mincing about like Minnie Caldwell.'

But when someone like the captain calls me Madame, I can ignore her snooty ways.

I managed to get to the bridge class just in time for her to collect me. She said, 'Have you had a lovely morning?' So I told her and she said nothing, just sighed, looking somewhere into the far distance.

On these cruises they don't let you bring alcohol on board. I like Amontillado mixed with a drop of Morrisons Medium Cream, so Pam put a litre and a half of ready mixed sherry into large lemonade bottles. She just carried them on. She's very clever at smuggling. I don't know where she gets these ideas from. Harry wasn't devious. Although it's as well that she did, because I always have a sherry and a packet of salt and vinegar crisps at half past twelve or I don't enjoy my dinner, or lunch as Pam calls it.

Well, I can't sit here enjoying myself for much longer. She'll come rampaging along any minute to drag me to Advanced Napkin Folding.

We'll be home tomorrow. That'll be lovely. I've got Wimbledon to look forward to, but not much else after that.

There's just Pam and me. We have no other family except her daughter Kirsten. Kirsten has two lovely children, Aimee and John, and a lovely husband, Marcus. They like to spend time alone. Especially at Christmas, *en famille* as they call it.

Pam and I will probably go to Scarborough again, drive onto the beach and have smoked salmon sandwiches and champagne.

I wish Harry had lived.

Revenge

Well, I mean to say, she really deserved it. She had it coming. There she is, twitching her curtains, tweaking her eyebrows, adjusting her bosom, but he won't come.

It all started in April. The weather was too hot too soon. I know all about tropical heat because once I went to Ibiza, with Wray's coaches. It were grand, but I couldn't live in heat like that, and no bingo neither.

Anyway, there was a duck on an island in the middle of our village pond. She had been sitting on her eggs for weeks and, one Tuesday – it must have been a Tuesday because it was shepherd's pie for tea – there were eight little ducklings, newly hatched. They were a bit wobbly, paddling fast in the water to keep up with mummy duck. Mummy and daddy were so proud of their brood. Beaks in the air, seeming to say, 'Just look what we've done.' They were lovely little things, pretty as a picture on an Easter card, all fluffy and yellow.

Well, Mabel and me, Mabel is the woman from next door, took to going every morning with some bread and a flask of tea. We were getting ready to go one day – it must have been a Monday because we'd just pegged out the washing – and Mabel said, 'Did you see that heron flying over? It looked to be heading straight for the pond.' Straight away, we dashed off and there it was: a heron, standing in the water, immobile, its beady eyes staring at our little darlings. If birds can slaver, that bird was slavering.

If I'd known then what I know now, I would have said there were two nasty birds beside the pond that day: Mabel and the heron. It was after our ducklings, that was plain. Both of us puffed up at this. Mabel, being more forthright than me, said, 'If that bloody bird thinks it's making a meal out of our babies, it's got another think coming.'

So we took it in turns to stay beside the pond every night to make sure all the chicks were safe and sound, not supper for that nasty bird.

It must have been a Friday – pension day – that Mabel saw an advert in the Yorkshire Post. It said something like, 'Company director would like to meet, etc, etc, for good times or more, GSOH, SWALK, that kind of thing.' I didn't like to ask what they meant. Knowing her, they're probably dirty, especially the 'or more' bit. She said, 'Gosh, he sounds a bit of alright. After all I've still got decent legs.' She's always had an inflated opinion of herself.

Anyway, that night Mabel went on a 'rondayvoos' with him, the chap from the advert.

She looked like mutton dressed as lamb, with thick make-up and six-inch heels that made her bottom stick out. The taxi arrived, and she tottered off, complete with a plastic rose pinned to her jacket. I expect she was meeting him under the town hall clock. It was her turn at duck watching, but I said I'd do a spell until she got back. She did come back, but not until morning.

When she landed at my house she looked like the cat who'd nicked the cream. A bit stiffly, I asked, 'Had a good time?'

She went all gooey. 'He was lovely. He had clean nails, a neat ponytail, and shiny shoes.'

He'd taken her to a 'beestrow' where there were candles in old Chianti bottles. I thought that was naff in the 60s, but didn't say anything.

The weeks passed by. The ducklings got bigger and lost their baby feathers. Mummy and daddy, or Liz and Philip as we called them, gave them lessons on how to dive under the water. We'd stopped guarding them at night because the heron had given up; the chicks were too big for him to take.

Mabel was seeing her 'chap' once or twice a week. Although she didn't confide in me, I'm sure they were at it like rabbits. Then came the week when he didn't ring. She tried to phone him, but there was no reply.

The next day she came into my kitchen and slapped a bag down on the table. 'What's that?'

'It's Gordon, we couldn't keep all those male ducks, they'd start fighting. Should we roast or stew him?'

I sat down with a thump, my head bursting, and screamed at her, 'What have you done? How could you? You are nothing but a hard and spiteful woman.' I burst into tears.

She was trying to tell me something, but I wasn't listening. Then she started shouting, 'Morrisons, Morrisons, I bought it at Morrisons.'

Well, it takes a lot for me to turn, but turn I did. It was the most cruel and spiteful thing anyone has ever done to me and I told her so. I threw her out. Good riddance.

That was yesterday. I didn't sleep all night. By this morning I'd had an idea. I dialled Mabel's number, put a hankie over the mouthpiece, and said in a nasal whine, 'Hello, is that Mrs Arkwright?'

'Yes, can I help you?' said Mabel in her telephone voice.

'I'm calling to say a man's been at my door asking where you live, so I told him. I hope that that was all right? What did you say? Yes, he did have a ponytail. He said he'll be with you in about five minutes. Goodbye.'

I was shaking when I put the phone down, but it serves her right. Her curtains have been twitching all day, but you know, and I know, he won't be coming.

Bees in the Catmint

I could catch bees in the pewter coffee jug and snap the hinged lid shut. I hid behind the sundial. The bees buzzed in the pot.

I didn't know Grandpa had taken a photograph until he showed me it in the album. I was hiding, not very well, with Blue Rabbit under one arm and, the coffee pot on the ground beside me, peeping round the sundial with my back to the camera. I loved the way Grandpa was always there to have fun, soothe me with a shiny sixpenny piece when I cried, or let me have the first choice of buns.

Grandfather was born in 1898. At sixteen he enlisted, at the start of what was to become known as The Great War, and was sent to join the German East Africa campaign. He never spoke of his experiences.

'It wasn't the same man that came back,' I heard Grandma telling her friends. I wondered what he could have been like before, and what was different about him?

Their home was surrounded by trees. A stream gurgled along the boundary. On long sunny summer afternoons, the grown-ups played croquet whilst we played hide and seek, floated paper boats on the pond and tried to find Bertie the badger. I had other friends besides bees and badgers. Butterflies, birds, and rabbits kept me occupied through the long summer holidays.

Grandma made egg sandwiches for Blue Rabbit and me. From our den under the cypress trees, we watched all that went on in the garden, and the comings and goings in the house. Sometimes we wished we were in one of the little planes that soared above, looping the loop, or leaving lazy patterns in the sky.

On rainy days we hid in the greenhouse. The rain coursed down the glass seams trying to get in, but we were snug in the muggy atmosphere. The smell of lilies, agapanthus and calendula was almost too delicious to bear. Drops of water seeped through a pinprick hole in the roof. Blue Rabbit and I watched as it found a path down the dark green leaves until it reached the point of no return and, like a pearl, dropped to the gravel floor. There were tomatoes as sweet as toffees and grapes that fizzed on the tongue. It was my job, as Grandpa's second-in-command, to make sure that everything was kept watered.

One day, as the rain poured down, I was reading Blue Rabbit a story, when the door to the greenhouse clicked open. It was Grandma.

'Are you in here? Have you seen Grandpa?'

We scuttled under a trestle table. Putting my finger to my lips, I whispered 'sssh' to Blue Rabbit.

Grandma had come to find us, bringing the dog with her. He was like Grandpa, old, and losing his hair, his walk a hop, skip and a jump, with rheumy eyes that stared into the far distance. The dog saw us, sat down and scratched his ear.

'Come and help me look for him, his uniform and gun are missing.'

Grandpa had a gun? We often played cowboys and Indians. Maybe he was waiting for me to join him. I was about to call out, but I knew where he would be. He wouldn't want a fuss. We would go to him, and bring him back for tea.

'Come on, dog, she's not here. We'll try the den.' The door clicked shut.

After the downpour a rainbow arched over the house, the light full of promise. We waited until Grandma had disappeared through the trees, crept out and headed towards the stream, slithering on the mud.

He would be near the willow. Its leaves trailed in the water like needy fingers, swirling the trout pools. We often went to the stream. It was where Grandpa had taught me to tickle trout. I cried the first time he pulled one out, its skin glistening like jewels. It was an initiation, from being a child to an adult. I didn't want to grow up.

Grandpa was there. Something was wrong. His face was smeared with mud, and he held the gun pointed at the far bank.

I tripped and dropped Blue Rabbit. Grandpa wheeled round and pointed the gun at me, his voice a clarion call.

'Captain, they're behind us.'

My Boy

A special Birthday, my boy's fortieth. The light of my life, the reason I am, the reason for everything that has happened in my life, and the only thing that makes anything worthwhile.

There he is. A bright blonde baby blowing bubbles at me, with the photographer saying, 'Yes, keep waving the rattle.' Click, click, click.

Look, there he it is on the sideboard. Wait a minute, I'll move the flowers so that you can see him better. The one next to it is the day he started to walk. Just see him. I wasn't expecting it to happen so soon, although they say boys are quicker than girls when it comes to walking. Those legs. His grandmother said he had the legs of Britain. Strong and straight, they would take him everywhere and anywhere he wanted.

One day I was polishing an old chest of drawers and didn't realise that a pair of chubby legs had walked past, at least not for a second. He was heading straight towards the front door, the sunshine, the steps and danger. I ran and scooped him into my arms. He laughed, throwing back his head as if to say, 'I did it. I've got the hang of that, what's next?'

I squeezed him hard to my chest, feeling the love pass between us, an overpowering need to wrap him in a protective shell that would never be broken. He smiled. We knew it would always be like this between us.

His first day at school, the black and white photograph on the mantelpiece next to the clock, do you see it? White shirt and striped tie, short grey trousers, blazer, socks and lace- up shoes, his cap slightly askew. I straightened it, turned him around and gently urged him towards the teachers waiting at the school door. I turned away, reluctant to join the other mothers chatting at the gate. I'd lost my boy, lost him to the system, entrusted him to the machine of state. How I wished to keep him close, to teach him how to protect himself from the tyranny of life, and show him beautiful things. How the seasons unfold; Winter sunshine slicing through leafless trees. The difference in summer when the light becomes dappled by the juicy greenness. The shadows when the horse chestnuts are ready. The slow shedding fall until the trees sleep again, waiting for the renaissance of spring.

He grew and grew like the chestnut tree. See, over there on the piano, his first day at big school. Long trousers, a lopsided smile, the world his oyster. The girls all fell for him, but he had no idea. He thought that everyone in the world was like him, self-effacing, with an excuse for anyone's shortcomings. He could be naughty but never in any way vindictive. He was mischievous too. I remember the time that he started the Duke of Edinburgh scheme, and I was so proud.

One morning the telephone rang and a very posh voice asked to speak to Mrs Hardisty.

'Speaking.'

'Hello, Mrs Hardisty. I am an equerry to the Duke of Edinburgh he would like a word with you, would that be convenient?'

Well, I smoothed down my pinafore, stood up straight, coughed, and said, 'I would be honoured, Your Grace.'

After all, it was such a shock. What else could I say? There was a pause on the line.

'Hello, Mrs Hardisty.'

I couldn't help myself, I curtsied. It didn't sound exactly like the Duke of Edinburgh but then I'd never spoken to him before.

'Your son will have told you that we are going camping to the Isle of Bute this weekend?'

'Oh yes, Your Majesty.'

'Please don't be formal. Philip will do. The problem is that we have no-one to look after the corgis. Could we, that is the Queen and I, drop them off with you for a couple of days?'

I hesitated for a moment. 'Well, er, of course, Your Highness. I can't see there being a problem.'

Howls of laughter came down the phone.

'Who is this? Is this a joke?'

I heard another wave of mirth Then the line went dead. The little tinker, wait till he gets home. I wasn't cross, though, I was pleased by his imagination and wit.

Naturally, he passed all his exams for Oxford, where he read something that I couldn't spell, and he met a lovely girl.

His face is fading, I cannot see it any longer. I must go and buy flowers before the night draws in. I always buy flowers for his birthday. When I get back, I will try to remember more. Did he get married or is he still a bachelor? It will come back to me when I dream.

Goodnight, my angel.

Beau

For two months there had been no respite from the sun scorching everything to toast. She'd had enough of the weather, and her job, making pasties at Greggs. That morning there had been a relentless queue since they opened, and they all wanted pasties. She'd spied Beau as she was adjusting the far from glamorous hairnet they all had to wear, wiping sweat from her brow. What the hell? She'd told him last night she never wanted to see him again.

She put the next batch of pasties in the oven, turned, and went behind the scenes without looking back. A few minutes later, she peeped into the shop, Beau was gone.

Emma had met Beau six months before, attracted by his disdain for conventional fashion. Plus, he didn't carry a phone like a talisman. He was tall and gangly, and flapped his arms when he spoke. He wore wonderfully strange, brightly-coloured, loose clothes, like an extrovert peacock. He worked at Butterfly Gardens.

She had been intrigued as he hopped from one topic to another. He wasn't like other lads, tongue-tied unless they'd had a drink or two, and then they only wanted one thing. She and Beau did things like going to the cinema, or for walks. He always sniffed flowers and weeds, and told her their Latin names. As well as knowing all the birds by their songs, he seemed to sense the weather. 'It's going to rain later,' he'd say. Or, 'You'll need a cardigan, it's going to get parky.'

Last night the inevitable had happened. Why had she thought he would be any different. They had been up at the tarn, the sun slowly sinking into the moors. The sky was streaked with all the colours of the rainbow. Birds chattered, ready to settle down for the night. The heat of the day was dying down, yet still warm like a soft blanket. Beau had an arm around her shoulders, a twinkle in his eye.

'Red sky at night, shepherds delight,' said Emma, trying to change the subject which seemed about to crop up.

'Isn't it amazing that the reason for this fabulous sky is the high density of dust particles.? It means high pressure, with air coming from the west. It'll be a fine day tomorrow.'

'How do you know these fascinating facts?'

'Instinct.'

He nuzzled her ear, Emma came over all tingly, but she didn't want that.

'Beau, please stop now. I've told you, I don't want that kind of relationship. Can't we be friends, good friends?'

'We could be lovers, and friends too.' He didn't stop nibbling.

Emma pushed him away, stood and turned her back towards him. 'Have you been leading me on all these months, being kind, apparently enjoying my company?

'I thought—'

'What exactly?'

Beau came to stand beside her. He picked up a pebble and threw it in a high arc towards the tarn, where it sank, leaving circles in the water. 'I thought you'd want to seal the deal.'

Emma erupted. 'Seal the deal. Is that what you call it? Go away, leave me alone.'

'You're making a big mistake, Emma. I'll never let you go.'

'Go.'

Beau sloped off down the hill, soon lost in the shadows. Beau rhymes with faux, she thought, a false friend.

Emma sat down. closed her eyes and sighed. She felt a shadow come over her. She opened her eyes to see Beau hovering, silhouetted by a strange aura. He was wearing a voluminous shirt of blue, red and green, iridescent in the dappled light. His face appeared thinner, his ears longer, pointed with nodules at the tips. He waved his arms. His feet seemed not to touch the ground.

'I told you that I'll never let you go, you're mine.'

Emma felt a stabbing pain in her groin. Beau laughed. His body lifted off and flew away. He shimmered towards the sunset.

Emma sat up, shaking her head. Silly girl, what a stupid dream. Flew away? As if, although it had seemed real. Emma walked back home listening to the birdsong, trying to keep her mind off what had happened.

A week later, Emma was taking a batch of pasties out of the oven when the stomach cramps hit. Her legs gave way.

'Lumme, what's up, lass?'

The women clustered around her, clucking like mother hens. Someone lifted her into the back of the shop.

'Open the door. Emma needs some air.'

Emma heard a bird screech as they laid her on the floor. She felt dizzy. Her tummy was doing somersaults. She tried to lift herself up. What was happening?

'Lie down Emma, relax. Oh, good heavens, call an ambulance quick. Emma's laying eggs.'

The Trip to the Gym

'Come on we're going to be late.'

'Are you sure it's a proper gym?'

Nanna pulls a face and doesn't bother to reply. I know better than to say anything. I'm staying with her for the weekend. At breakfast she said, 'I've booked an appointment at a gym. It's about time you did something physical instead of spending hours on your Ybox.'

'Xbox.'

'Ybox, Xbox. whatever. When I was a girl you didn't find me inside playing games.' Nanna launched into one of her endless stories of the dark ages. They always started with 'when I was a girl'. Bollocks, I thought, but not out loud, as the last time I'd said it Nanna gave me a clatter that made my head ring.

When she ran out of steam, she went back to explaining about the gym, 'You'll need a towel for the showers, there might even be a pool, and you'll need trainers.'

Now, in a run-down bit of town, Nanna swerves into a Tesco car park.

'Why've you stopped?'

'I spotted the sign. Look, it's over there.'

A small hand-painted arrow points up a mucky, cobbled ginnel. The buildings are derelict or barricaded with razor wire. The gym has a rusty girder structure propping up the outer walls. The entrance door is dented and dirty, the sagging staircase up to the first floor is steep and mucky. Sounds of scuffling feet, grunts and groans come from above. How did Nanna find this dump? It looks like she googled 'dodgy drug dealing den'.

'Nanna, are we in the right place? It doesn't look like a proper gym. Do I have to go in, can't I wait in the car while you see if it's OK?'

'It does look a bit grim, but at least we should go in and have a look. Charlotte is expecting us.'

At the top of the creaky stairs there is a corridor. Half way along we find a door with *gym* painted in wonky letters. The door creaks open. A person comes to meet us and shakes Nanna's hand then mine, almost crushing my fingers.

'Hello, I'm Charlotte.'

It's a woman?

She has a six pack like Stallone, with huge, knotted biceps that look as though they've had a bicycle pump at work on them. She is wearing black shorts with lace-up boots, and has the shadow of a moustache. She's scary.

Her photos are all over the walls. Pimply kids, all lads, are knocking shit out of one another. The floor is old lino with holes. and the ceiling is held up with loopy pink plastic. At the far side of the 'gym' is a boxing ring and several punch bags. No sign of showers, never mind a pool.

'Must go to the toilet.' I make a dash down the corridor. I can smell the bog before I get there, it stinks. A sign above the sink reads *Clean up blood before leaving.* I stand outside the door into the gym, unwilling to go back in. The door opens.

'Nanna, there's a sign in the loo that says clean up blood—'

Behind her, Charlotte interrupts, 'That's because noses bleed easily if they get bumped.'

She folds her arms. biceps taut.

'Do you want to learn how to box? Because to be involved in a sport you must co-operate. It's all to do with teamwork. Are you coming back next Saturday to start training?' she asks, so close to my face I can almost feel her moustache waggling.

I mutter yes without looking up. I'd rather load my pockets with bricks and jump in the River Wharfe.

'Thank you, Charlotte, we'll see you next week.' says Nanna and shakes her hand, smiling as though she means it.

Nanna whispers, 'Say thank you.'

We are almost back to the car when Nanna grabs me in a bear hug.

'Sorry, chicken. That was awful.'

'What, you're not cross with me?'

'No, I realised as soon as we got inside that it wasn't the sort of gym that you wanted. I didn't want to stay, but it would have been rude to leave straightaway. What about if next week we go to a Morris dancing class, fencing, drama or pottery?'

'Boring. How about The New Mutants film and then McDonalds?'

'When I was a girl...'

Oh, Gawd, she's off again.

'...I used to swing over the river on a bit of rope, and go pot-holing or hang gliding. Exciting things.' We're out of the car park and on the ring road again before she says, 'Did I tell you I'm starting a motorcycling course? I've always fancied a large, black, throbbing motorbike.'

All my mates have nannas that work in charity shops, or help the homeless. They have perms and scabby lap dogs to walk in the park – but not my grandmother.

If only she was normal.

Other Publications by Chapeltown Books

Tripping the Flash Fantastic
by Allison Symes

Allison Symes loves reading and writing quirky fiction. She discovered flash fiction thanks to a Cafélit challenge and has been hooked on the form ever since. In this follow-up to her *From Light to Dark and Back Again*, Allison will take you back in time, into some truly criminal minds, into fantasy worlds, and show you how motherhood looks from the viewpoint of a dragon. Enjoy the journey!

"Fabulous collection of poems and flash fiction. Some made me giggle, some made me gasp, all surprised me! Highly recommend this!" *(Amazon)*

Order from Amazon:
ISBN: 978-1-910542-58-3 (paperback)
978-1-910542-59-0 (ebook)

Chapeltown Books

The World in an Eye
by Maroula Blades

The World In An Eye is an eclectic collection. It ardently and boldly tackles issues that plague our societies. Presenting diverse flash fiction stories set in America, England, Germany, Italy and other places where poignancy, rawness and sensitivity are propelled to the foreground. This evocative compilation also thrusts taboo topics out from the fringes into the spotlight. Here, they explore and expose the lives of those not fed with golden spoons.

"A moving and haunting collection of short stories. Rich poetic words and thought provoking narrative. Take your own time and drink it in. Beautiful." *(Amazon)*

Order from Amazon:
ISBN: 978-1-910542-56-9 (paperback)
978-1-910542-57-6 (ebook)

Chapeltown Books

Theme and Variations
by Vanessa Horn

Theme and Variations is a collection of sixteen flash fiction stories with music – some of it harmonious, some discordant – running through them.

Although fictional, these stories also contain many elements of realism. After all, music will always be with, around or in you.

Order from Amazon:
ISBN: 978-1-910542-51-4 (paperback)
978-1-910542-52-1 (ebook)

Chapeltown Books

www.ingramcontent.com/pod-product-compliance
Lightning Source LLC
Chambersburg PA
CBHW080754120626
46557CB00005B/1261